Look What They Have Turned Me Into

Randolph Marks

Copyright © 2024

All Rights Reserved

Dedication

I dedicate this book to my four babies—Maria, Axel, Allan and Ignacio—the Marks family.

To my brother, Micky Marks, who always checks up on my progress on this book.

My little sister Amrita Marks, we don't see each other very often, but you are always included in everything.

To my little sister, Sherry Marks, we have a Tom and Jerry relationship, but I know you will always be there for me as I am always there for you.

Thanks to Jennifer Charles for helping nourish this idea.

My mom, Shirreem Baijnath, always supports me in everything I do.

Thanks to my best friend, Jayshree Rahman, for always being there for me through the good and bad times.

A special thank you to Vishnunarine Singh, aka Uncle Cheese, who's always been there for me since I was a little kid.

This book is also dedicated to everyone out there who has always wanted to write a book but has never had the opportunity to do so. Keep writing. Anything is possible as long as you put your mind to it.

Lastly, I also dedicate it to all fiction lovers. I hope you all have chills while reading this.

Acknowledgment

All thanks to Allah for blessings and knowledge.

I would like to acknowledge my family, Shireen Baijnath, Rudolph Marks, Mickey Marks, Sherry Marks and Amrita Marks for their continuous support.

I'd like to thank my children, Maria, Axel, Allan and Ignacio for being my strength.

To my friends, Nordia Morrison, Jayshree Rahiman, Bob Warner, and Larry Warner for always being there for me.

In loving memory of Haresh Shivambar (Devin) and Sahid Hamid, you guys are greatly missed!

Special thanks to Jennifer Charles for constantly encouraging me.

About the Author

A Guyanese-American and father to four beautiful kids, Randolph Marks is passionate about fiction. He believes fiction is a work of art, and our brain is an amazing organ that can take us to imaginary places no matter where we are. Life is like a dream, and amusingly, a dream is like a movie, and we can be a part of it, which makes it worth it.

Randolph Marks firmly believes that there are only two ways to live your life. One is as though *nothing is a miracle*, and the other is as though *every thing is a miracle*.

The fact that we are here in a human body is said to be a one in four hundred trillion chance. Very few of us believe that we are a walking miracle. Still, sadly, many people are walking around living in their heads, being pessimistic about the future and bitter about the past, so much so that they are missing the miracles in the present.

Contents

Dedication i

Acknowledgment ii

About the Author ii

Chapter 1: Innocence Lost 1

Chapter 2: Seeds of Resentment 9

Chapter 3: The First Kill 15

Chapter 4: A Deadly Occupation 27

Chapter 5: The Joy of Killing 38

Chapter 6: Lessons Learned In Blood 45

Chapter 7: Seeking Redemption 58

Chapter 8: Embracing Darkness 66

Chapter 9: Reaching Out for Help 74

Chapter 10: Facing Justice 82

Chapter 11: The Final Price 85

Chapter 1: Innocence Lost

Being associated with a particular race, I know what it feels like when you have to face hate from people around you, even when you have done nothing wrong other than just existing and trying to build a future for yourself. There are thousands of people in the world who bear racialism daily, yet they have no choice but just to ignore it and move on. But this just doesn't end there, and the cycle goes on! It comes at you at different places and different times.

My name is Randy, and I am an Afro-American. I have lived in South America since I was born in Guyana. It is one of the least populated countries on the surface of the earth, with a population of only around 813,000 people. Guyana is a local word that means *Land of Many Waters*. The population consists of native people who speak English and the native Guyanese Creole language, also known as Creolese. It is a beautiful country containing numerous rivers, streams, and their small tributaries, thus being called the *Land of Many Waters*. Many tribal people are inhibited here, and almost 30% of the native population includes Black people.

I had always wanted to move to the United States since my early childhood. As far as I remember, I have never wanted to be in Guyana. It was like a dream; I had always wished to live a better life in the States. I couldn't wait for the time when I would move and live in the US. I was always so eager to learn everything about it. I learned about their culture, traditions, life, and people. I would imagine adjusting there and trying to be a better version of myself before going there.

I have been an energetic and objectively good kid since my childhood. I had many dreams and ambitions while growing up. I tried to focus on my studies and my personality. As I grew up, I tried to become a better person and a polished version of myself every day. I had always been a kind, ambitious, and hardworking boy. I was open-minded and could acquire new skills and knowledge with a passion to do something significant.

Then, one day, I finally got to move to the US. It felt like a dream coming into reality, and I felt delighted. I traveled there as an immigrant at first. If I spoke honestly, I felt a void in my heart to leave my country and relocate, but I didn't forget that it had been my ambition forever. I had to suppress my emotions so they didn't come in the way of my goal. I would convince myself that this is happening for a reason and reassure myself that it is for the best. I had high hopes before leaving for America. I wanted to live the best life there and avail myself of every opportunity. I was determined to work very hard and was ready to take any chance I would get. I strongly felt that something good might happen to me over there, as I was confident about my objectives. I had already planned my life in America. I had everything figured out in my mind that I wanted to accomplish in the States.

I settled in Schenectady with my family. It was a small suburban city on the outskirts of Schenectady County in New York State, with many lakes and beaches. We rented a small, old house that was located near Mariaville Lake. It was a dull and conventional city. There were very few exciting things to do there. Life was slow, simple, and plain. It was not a very safe place to live either, with a not-so-secure environment. However, we settled there initially. We started a new life there from scratch. I sometimes felt out of place, as it was a completely new place. But I had promised myself that I would never give up and always remember my ambition.

I came to know that many Guyanese people were living in Schenectady. They were more in number in Schenectady than in their own country, Guyana! They did not speak very fluent English; they spoke broken English with a British accent due to its association with Britain as a colony in the past. I want to mention how beautiful Guyanese people are; they are kindhearted, hardworking, and brave.

From what I remember, the literacy rate was very high. Children went to school because education was necessary as per government law. The natives mostly worked as teachers, civil officers, and other professionals. However, most of the Guyanese people lived below the poverty line. There were very few opportunities other than fishing, cultivation, and agriculture. So, people looked for chances for employment and a good education elsewhere, mostly in the US. Many Guyanese white-collar workers, such as doctors and other trained professionals, emigrated. However, Guyanese locals were interested in sports, especially cricket, boxing, football, table tennis, and squash.

Other than that, Guyanese people lived in ethnic groups and had very cordial relationships among them.

After moving to Schenectady, I went to a nearby elementary school, and following that, I attended a high school. Growing up, I thought of different pursuits to follow as my future endeavors. Like any other kid, I also had so many ambitions that I couldn't decide on one. At times, I wished to be a pilot and wanted to fly planes. And then, sometimes, I would think of becoming a police officer and helping people in their various matters and predicaments. I yearned to eradicate every crime surfacing around us. I also considered becoming a detention officer and serving the state's justice system. I would also consider becoming a bus or race car driver. I sometimes even considered joining the Air Force and becoming a jet pilot.

I also joined *the Junior Reserve Officer's Training Corps* (JROTC). This military development program for high school students helped shape my personality and enhance my leadership skills. It helped me build confidence and discipline in my character. Growing up, I was always focused on working on my self-growth in every way possible. I had always been working hard and was open to learning new things. I learned to paint and knit clothes. I tried to do or learn every new skill I liked, and I enjoyed doing that. I wanted to learn everything and acquire every bit of knowledge I could!

I was determined to stay updated with everything and wanted to keep moving forward. I knew this new place had so much to offer me, and I wanted to make the most of it. I wanted to be at the top!

Besides everything else, I was a sympathetic guy. I had a soft heart and possessed kindness and compassion toward others. I wanted to help kids with physical disabilities and various mental disorders. I wished to be of any help to them in any possible way and wished to provide them assistance. I didn't want to see anyone suffering through disabilities and pain.

But little did I know that the new place had other plans for me. I was unaware of all the realities as a kid; I just focused on my ambitions and goals, and while strategizing them, I ignored the fact that I could be subjected to hate, too. I had no idea what it would be like to live in a new place as an immigrant, and that too as a Black guy!

Along with seeking and learning so much in my early life, I noticed some strange patterns in my behavior. I realized that I had a problem with my temper and something was wrong in my brain. I had bipolar disorder and observed sudden changes in my temper and mood. Occasionally, I would notice unusual changes in my emotional state, temperament, energy levels, and activities. It would feel like I was not in the right frame of mind. Nevertheless, I would control myself and keep moving forward. I didn't let this issue hinder the track I had chosen!

I had high expectations before coming to America and was determined to meet them eventually. However, one of the problems that I faced after moving to the States was racial discrimination. I had to face endless hate only because I was a Black guy. Being new there and a kid, I could not fathom why a set of people hated me only because of the color of my skin. I thought it was absurd, which it actually was.

How could somebody hate a human being for a factor not even under his control? And, how did the color of one's skin make a difference to anyone to the extent that they hated them so much?

However, I kept living there while continuously facing hate and discrimination. Everyone around me was white-skinned. All of my friends, teachers, neighbors, and peers were White. Since my adolescence, I have been interested in people from other races and have been keen to get to know them. I liked talking to them and befriending them. I liked White people, yet the most hate I experienced was from White people!

School was the place where the bullying started; my classmates would laugh at me and bully me during class. I performed well in school but never got as much recognition as compared to the White kids. I was hated in the local area where I lived. No one played with me while I was growing up. Then, I went to college and faced the same bias. I missed out on good chances and opportunities my whole life just because I was Black, which was ridiculous! I was refused many job opportunities, and White people were given preference over me despite my skills and abilities.

I was constantly made fun of! Local Americans around me used to laugh at how I spoke. Although I spoke reasonably good English, people would not spare me despite that. They would sometimes stare at me in the streets like I was some sort of alien. At times, this treatment made me extremely furious, and I even wanted to fight back. I despised the way I was treated because I looked different from the White people, which is why I had to go through so many awful experiences as well.

Although I wasn't the only one having such experiences, many other Black people around me faced this hate. We all had relatable experiences and encounters with the White locals. Surprisingly, they didn't even spare the local Black Americans, and they were also treated the same way as us. Because of this prejudice, people around me doubted my abilities regardless of my skills, expertise, and dedication. They used to show prejudice and treat me differently than the White kids, especially in high school.

Such incidents would probably affect anyone facing them; I was affected, but I never let that consume me for long. It greatly affected my self-esteem even though I stayed focused on my ambition and always reminded myself what I was there for. I went through many uncomfortable situations that tore down my confidence, but I continued the path I decided on. I tried my best to stay strong and confident and did not allow the hardships to stop me from moving forward.

As I reflect on everything that happened to me, I believe that it taught me to stay strong and consistent throughout my childhood and adulthood. I ignored the many stones thrown at me. I tried to ignore people who desired to bring me down. Instead, I surrounded myself with people who wished me well. Some days, I felt like I was not in the right state of mind and wished to give up. However, I didn't want to give up on my dream of living and growing up in America. I did not want to go back to Guyana! That is why, throughout these difficult years, I tried to navigate my life, facing all the bumps just to achieve what I had in my mind for myself. So, I didn't lose hope and stayed there despite all the difficulties.

Facing racial discrimination was really tough, and it messed up my mind and my personality. It could bring life-long traumas to those who face it. No matter what you do or how much you try to be the best version of yourself, you can still be subjected to hate and bigotry if you are an outlander or have a darker skin color. This is what moving to the States taught me; it was totally different from what I imagined.

Chapter 2: Seeds of Resentment

Racism became a part of my existence. As I look back, I can remember that it never came to an end—instead, I grew up with it. Left, right, or center, everywhere I would go, there would be racism, welcoming me with open arms. Accepting and taking it as a challenge was the worst part, as I had no choice. Whatever I did, I was unable to avoid it. Sometimes, it seemed like it had become my fate, and I had to endure it at every cost.

Recalling my high school phase makes me wonder if I have ever had any joyful moments, and we know that high school is the most ecstatic phase of an adolescent's life. But for me, it was very different. Nobody in my school stood up for me when I faced racism. The worst part was receiving no support from my teachers because most of them were White.

All through middle and high school, there was no one in whom I could confide. However, many others like me were victims of racism and discrimination, and I resonated with them, but what I needed was a *friend*. And speaking honestly, I had no one I could call a friend!

The sound of people laughing at me still echoes in my ears, and I can clearly remember every moment and memory of when they ridiculed me. I can still see people around me laughing, pointing fingers at me, making fun of me, and considering me like a clown. Every moment would hurt like hell, but I continued my life despite that.

My daily life had become a struggle. I dreaded leaving the house and didn't want to become a laughingstock for passersby. Sometimes, I wondered what I had done wrong to make people treat me like that. I wondered how people were inconsiderate and insensitive to hurt others for no reason. In addition, I questioned myself about what I did wrong that enabled others to make me feel less human, even though I knew I did nothing wrong.

I reckon it was not me that was the problem, but rather the people. While growing up in the US, I never did anything wrong or committed any crime, but it was the people who turned me into a monster!

As I moved forward in my life, I developed hate and resentment toward everybody who treated me like dirt. I loathed every human being around me, and my inclination toward white people turned into resentment.

The feelings of hatred, abomination, and resentment only progressed over time. I knew it was wrong on my behalf, but it was already too late. By then, the situation was out of my control, and I had lost control over myself.

Everything that happened to me changed who I was. I had developed an inner voice who I talked to, expressed what I felt, and shared what I went through the day. It was because I had lost faith in humanity and remained in my bubble. I named my inner voice *Jason* and spent nights talking to it. It was the only thing that listened to me and passed no judgment. Jason became my best friend, and I confided in him with the progression.

I nearly stopped talking to anyone around me and remained occupied by my inner voice. I became numb and heartless to an extent when the bullying stopped bothering me anymore.

You would think I was healing. But no…! it worsened the situation for me. After facing any mistreatment or cruelty from people, I talked to Jason and vented out, and he became an outlet. Every time that happened, I felt lighter and less bothered. I would share with Jason how I wanted to treat people the same way they treated me. I expressed the resentment and hate that had built inside of me and how it ignited a spark of revenge.

Jason listened to me and never shut me off, which was the best thing that happened since I had never retaliated. I wasn't brave enough to do that. The fear instilled in me of what would happen if I ever reacted to it. It occurred due to losing my self-confidence at a very young age and never having the chance to regain it. And as a young boy in his developmental stages, it was the most terrible thing to happen.

Meanwhile, Jason stayed with me and became a confidant. He talked to me whenever I needed him and replied in my favor. I cursed and swore at people and wished them bad luck. I never dared to tell them to their faces, but I only disclosed my secret inner feelings to Jason. He would listen and encourage me to do as I pleased, and that would calm me down instantly.

A pattern was set just like that, and my anger and hate increased. The frustration that had accumulated inside me would be released after each session with Jason. And soon, Jason began to echo in my head. He made me realize that I craved revenge.

Shortly after my encounter with Jason, the fire inside me to take vengeance escalated. Every time something happened or whenever someone bullied me, I would return to Jason, and he would push me for an act of revenge. By then, I began to wish harm on people.

Changes in my behavior were evident, and I knew that I had changed. The sweet, innocent boy who came to the US to make progress for himself was lost and had turned into a monster who wanted to kill people who did him dirty.

Patience, tolerance, and self-restraint had disappeared from my personality, and I had turned into a maniac. My anger had increased, and I had become short-tempered. I lashed out at people who would bully me. The hate, anger, and frustration accumulated within me caused me to react and retaliate. This behavior resulted in heated arguments, quarrels, and assaults.

The physical and mental violence resulted in the escalation of my anger and frustration, and as a result, the hate and resentment inside me increased exceedingly. However, talking to Jason would help me in such circumstances, and I calmed down for a brief period. But the calm was short-lived because the bullying would never stop.

It became like a daily struggle for me to battle my inner thoughts. I knew my feelings were valid but not legitimate, and I had to set them right. Jason echoed in my mind frequently and assured me of how I felt and what I thought was not invalid and justified them. I felt like he was the only one who cared about me in this world, and there was no one else whom I could turn to unleash.

I remember an encounter with a man who harassed me on the bus because of my skin color. That was the first time I expressed something intense to Jason, thinking that he might tell me it was wrong because I knew that what I was thinking wasn't something I should be very proud of. Despite that, he validated it and instigated me. That was the point that provoked me to think of carrying out such heinous acts.

It took me a very long time to reach the extent of thinking to kill somebody. For the longest time, I battled with my subconscious to avoid the harassers and bullies and maintain my innocence. After all, I was not an evil man from the beginning, and my gut told me to stop.

Numerous times, I thought about hitting somebody or choking them to death. But somehow, I constrained myself and avoided involving myself in criminal acts. Moreover, I knew what it would get me into if I did something criminal; the fact that I was a Black immigrant added to the odds.

When these thoughts started emerging, the restlessness I felt was inexplicable. The constant frustration and resentment agitated me, which made things worse. I tried my best not to do anything that would turn against me or make me a monster. I wanted to remain innocent and live my life like a normal, customary human being because my roots were virtuous, and I resonated with them.

The constant battle I faced with my subconscious and conscience made it extremely difficult to carry out my daily tasks. Everywhere I went, I remained preoccupied and lost in my thoughts, paying no attention to my surroundings, and any mishap or mistreatment would only add to the chaos already boiling within me.

No one extended me any support or help when I needed it the most, resulting in me only leaning on Jason when I felt low. I could control myself for a while, but I knew that the resentment, anger, and frustration would result in something terrible one day!

Chapter 3: The First Kill

I had descended into a dark phase, from which it was nearly impossible to get out. My will to maintain my innocence, conscience, and morals had diminished, and all that I just wished was revenge!

I was not atrocious characteristically; the circumstances I was exposed to revealed a darker side of my personality. Every human being has a darker side, which might be undiscovered, but it can reveal itself when one is continuously exposed to prejudice and hatred.

Moreover, I am not sure if my behavior was justifiable, but I couldn't ignore the fact that it was out of control. Besides controlling myself and constraining my thoughts, I knew it would lead me to a dead end, and I would be stranded.

Jason—my inner voice, stayed with me for the whole time when I was devastated because of the bullying and racism. Jason was my friend, confidant, and savior, who turned me into something I had never imagined.

I had become comfortable talking to him, expressing my emotions, and venting my suppressed frustration, which had built up over time. I liked how Jason validated my thoughts and feelings and never judged me for them. Instead, Jason helped me navigate my feelings and process my emotions. I had become addicted to how Jason responded to me without interruptions. It seemed like he lived in my head rent-free, all the time, and was available at any moment of the day.

The time finally came when I bought a gun. I had no idea what I would do with it or how I would operate it, but my intuition made me get it. The moment I got my hands on it, I felt like I could make a difference for myself. For the first time, I felt powerful, and the dynamics changed instantly.

I bought the gun discreetly and went home that day. I went into my room, hiding the gun from my family, and shut the door. My heart was beating fast, and I could feel it thumping out of my chest. I was breathing heavily, and sweat was dripping down my forehead. I sat on my bed and took out the gun from the bag. I looked at the holster carefully, admiring its texture, and then took out the gun from it.

The moment I took out the gun from its holster, I thought, *Yes, now I am going to change the circumstances for myself.* The thought of taking revenge on every person who bullied me and the ones who might try to harass me in the future made me feel mighty. After looking closely at the gun for a while, I put it back inside the holster and placed it safely in my cupboard.

I felt a strange sense of relief, which I had never felt before, after coming to the US. I slept peacefully that night like a baby and woke up extremely fresh the next morning. I couldn't comprehend what was happening to me or how a gun could bring me such relief and help me regain my lost self-confidence. I couldn't ignore that feeling, so I kept wondering.

I had planned to make good use of the gun. Everyone who would possibly cause me any harm or any type of inconvenience would face my wrath. I was sure what they had turned me into, and I knew that I would not spare anyone from now on.

Furthermore, Jason was there with me. The voice kept echoing in my mind, instigating me to act and react because it was too much, and I had had enough. I would talk to Jason and ask for his reassurance. His validation gave me strength, and I knew I was ready to retaliate. I had planned everything and was prepared to execute it.

The young Randy, who was innocent and naive, had gotten lost somewhere. In his absence, I was going to avenge every single person who hurt and bullied him when he was a teenager and wasn't brave enough to take a stand for himself. I had vowed to take vengeance for every harassment and bullying that the young Randy had faced.

My emotions were intense, and I was sure that I wouldn't be able to control them anymore if something terrible happened. However, I wished nothing would happen that would lead me to do this heinous act.

Since the day I bought the gun, nothing happened for a couple of weeks. I was happy I didn't get a chance to do something criminal, but I knew this happiness wouldn't last long. Meanwhile, my inner voice, Jason, echoed inside me and kept reminding me of my motive. He would repeat that the peace and calm were short-lived—he was so right!

I vividly remember the first time I killed someone. I can still feel its essence. I remember every detail of my crime and how I felt after committing it. It was 9:00 p.m. on a Monday, and I was headed to the grocery store close to my house. There was pin-drop silence since not many people were there on the street. I drove to the store and parked at a distance. I went inside the store, picked up everything I needed, and went to the counter to pay for the items I had picked. Quickly, I paid at the counter and left the store.

Walking toward my car, I noticed somebody was following me. I turned back and saw two White men following me, who might be native Americans. The guy who was in the front robbed me and took everything I had in my wallet. He took all the cash I had and even the credit cards. I retaliated and fought him, but he was powerful and had a knife. He threatened me with the knife—I was helpless and had no other choice but to let go of my money.

He robbed everything and ran away with the other guy who didn't rob me but didn't stop his friend either. I figured out that they both were friends. All the while, when I was trying to defend myself, the guy who stood there didn't try to stop his friend from robbing me. No one else was present on the street at that moment who could have helped me from getting robbed.

The incident made me furious, so I went back home. I was fuming with anger. If I had taken my gun with me, I would have killed both of the muggers right on the spot. I was disappointed because I couldn't defend myself and felt like a failure. I was ashamed that I couldn't get myself out of a situation I had been prepared for. After all, I bought the gun to use during such an event, but I left it at home that night.

I stayed awake the whole night, and overthinking the robbery made me extremely restless. I knew I wouldn't calm down until I took revenge for my loss and the humiliation I faced. I was devastated. And then, I knew what I had to do as I remembered the face of the other guy, who stood at the back and watched everything happening right before his eyes, yet he remained unbothered. He could have stopped his friend from robbing me, but he didn't. I remembered his face clearly, and I knew I had to take revenge on him, and he would pay for everything that happened that day.

The next day, I went to the same grocery store at night. I stood there in a corner where no one could see me. I looked for that guy. I waited several hours before finally spotted him at the corner of the street.

"Ah! There I found him," I exclaimed in my mind.

I knew what I had to do next. I waited at the same spot until he turned his back and started walking in the opposite direction. Then, I started following him, making sure that he didn't notice me, or else everything would go down the drain.

I followed him secretly until he reached his home.

"Yes, I got it!' I exclaimed in my mind again.

I was delighted I had obtained what I had thought of getting... his address! Yes, I got his address—I knew where he lived. The first part of my plan had worked, and it already felt like an accomplishment.

I returned home, and my achievement for the day helped me sleep peacefully that night. I was happy that I could take revenge now. I was so excited that I couldn't wait any longer.

The next morning, I woke up feeling refreshed and recharged. I was determined to take my revenge the same day. I was so electrified that I couldn't wait patiently for the day to turn into night.

I waited and did my usual tasks for the day. As soon as the clock hit 7:00 pm, I took my gun out and looked at it closely. I held it in my hand, felt its texture, and admired how it would soon help me. I cleaned it with a paper towel and placed it back in the holster. I carefully placed the gun on my dresser and went to have dinner in the dining hall, closing the door of my room.

Shortly after dinner, it was 9:00 pm already. I went inside my room, picked up my gun, and left my house. I reached the same spot I went to yesterday and waited for the guy to appear while sitting in my car.

Within a few minutes, I spotted him at the corner of the street. I could feel my heart pounding; I was nervous, but I controlled myself, stayed determined, and focused on my plan.

I noticed the guy started walking in another direction. I waited and expected him to turn and go toward his house, which was in the opposite direction. But to my surprise, he continued to walk ahead, which I hadn't anticipated.

It looked like everything I had planned had become useless, and my excitement for vengeance was useless anymore. My heart dropped, and a feeling of hopelessness was evident. I was anxious about what I would do next and looked at my gun in despair.

I took a second to compose myself and suddenly had a revelation! I knew what I had to do now. I stepped out of my car and followed him with a pistol inside my jacket. He was ahead of me, and I tip-toed my way through so he wouldn't notice me.

To my surprise, he turned right on the street where I lived. As soon as I noticed this, I became nervous. My house was not far away from the spot he was walking on. Nevertheless, I kept my calm and kept stalking him.

Following him for five minutes, I had planned to attack him now. I paced up and grabbed him from behind, gripping his neck forcefully. Within a matter of seconds, I knocked him down on the street. I made sure that no one was watching me, and I also covered my face with a handkerchief and a black cap on my head that covered almost half of my forehead.

The street was completely silent, and no one was present nearby, which was a favorable factor for me. I had expected to kill him within a few seconds but didn't anticipate that he would get defensive. As soon as I knocked him down on the street, he kicked me in my gut. I was taken aback, and it hurt terribly. I stopped for a couple of seconds to comprehend what had happened, but he stood up and punched me in the face. Dang! Spark flashed before my eyes, and I felt dizzy. I heard his footsteps receding and figured that he had started running.

I did not want that to happen, so I returned to my senses and ran after him. He had not run very far away, and I caught him in seconds, grabbing him from the back of his neck with my arm. This time, I made sure not to leave any loopholes in my attack. I choked his neck with my right arm and punched him in his stomach with my left fist. I punched him repeatedly in his stomach until he fell on the floor on his knees. I knew that this was the moment.

I found a ray of hope at that moment and started punching him on the left side of his abdomen. I threw him on the floor and kicked him until he was almost unconscious. He was lying on the street with his eyes closed and motionless. I stared at him for a brief second and then took my gun out of my jacket.

At first, I aimed at his right leg and pulled the trigger. He screamed in pain as the bullet pierced through his thigh. He was trembling with pain, and I kept on looking at him. I knew that he was going to die soon. I had no sympathy for him because he did the same with me. He had a family, and I knew this. I knew he had two little kids and a young wife, yet my heart didn't melt, and I kept looking at him heartlessly and with a wicked smile. I felt extremely proud of myself, watching him beg for his life and knowing that I was going to kill him in just a few minutes.

He begged for his life, but I didn't show any mercy. I proceeded to choke his neck until he gagged. Moving on, I poked his eyes until he shouted at the top of his lungs. I wasn't worried if anyone would watch me taking his life in the middle of the street. I was sure that my face wasn't visible and nobody would be able to recognize me.

At that moment, I felt powerful. The thought of taking revenge made me feel like more than just a human.

Meanwhile, I kept saying, "You deserve it!"

I picked up my gun again and stood up, aiming at his forehead. I placed my index finger on the trigger and took a deep breath. The next moment, I pulled the trigger and watched the bullet piercing through his forehead and a stream of fresh blood flowing down his face.

I ran from the crime scene and came back to my car. I sat there in silence and took a sigh of relief. Before returning to the car, I removed the cap and mask from my face and threw them in the trash bin at the corner of the street. I looked around the area to make sure that no one was there when I killed the guy.

My heart was pounding, and I was out of breath. It took a few minutes to calm myself down, then I started the engine and drove home. I took an alternate route to reach my house to avoid getting into trouble.

Soon, I reached home, went inside my room, and put my pistol carefully inside the cupboard. Lying on the bed, I kept thinking about what I had just done. A weird sense of relief and pride had accumulated inside me, and I couldn't stop smiling. It was an achievement for me that I had finally taken revenge for myself, which I should have done sooner.

Moving on, I had a very good night's sleep and woke up feeling refreshed and cheerful the next morning. I didn't have any remorse or guilt for what I had done and continued with my tasks for the day like nothing unusual happened the previous night. I walked up and down the street, went to the grocery store, and even walked in the neighborhood. I wasn't scared at all and didn't care for any consequences.

Just by the middle of the day, the news of the crime was all over the television. The police were searching for the murderer and were looking for any suspects or clues. That didn't bother me at all. I wondered what had happened to me that I didn't feel anxious. I knew that maybe all of the trauma I had endured while growing up made me heartless, and that was the reason why nothing bothered me anymore. My inner voice echoed inside me, assuring me that I didn't do anything wrong and that he deserved it after what he did to me the night I got robbed.

The police searched the whole area and interrogated anyone that they found suspicious. I was aware that soon it would be my turn for the interrogation, and I was mentally prepared for it or anything worse that could happen to me.

The next morning, my doorbell rang, and I went out to check who it was. There, the policemen stood, looking directly at me. I was not quite surprised because I knew this moment would come sooner rather than later.

Keeping myself calm, I asked the policeman, "What is the matter?"

He explained the crime that happened in my vicinity, and I pretended to be oblivious to it. They asked me if I could provide the CCTV recording of the surveillance cameras installed outside my house.

I looked at them sternly and said without hesitation, "It's for my private business. It's not for the police, and it's not for the government. This is my personal CCTV."

The police begged for assistance, but I declined their request straight away. I was smiling inside, thinking they were asking the criminal himself for assistance in solving the crime he had committed. I asked them to go away, closing the door in their faces.

I could see the live recording of my yard being played on the television. The police were still standing there, looking around, perplexed and figuring out what they were going to do next. I went to open the door again and glared at them. I asked them again very rudely to leave my house and not roam around here. I slammed the door, came inside, and watched the news of the murder I committed, which was over every local news channel.

After everything happened, I sat on my couch in solitude while Jason echoed at the back of my mind. My heart was numb, and I couldn't feel anything. It looked like I had become apathetic, and nothing affected me anymore.

The feeling after committing my first murder increased the yearning for more. At that moment, I knew it wasn't just it, and there was much more to come!

Chapter 4: A Deadly Occupation

A couple of weeks passed by, but the police were unable to figure out that the criminal was just around the corner. Committing the murder very precisely, I left no clue behind for me to be caught.

Meanwhile, I lived my life peacefully, staying least bothered with what I did a few weeks ago. Not a single part of me felt any guilt or remorse for my actions. However, it now felt like an addiction; my heart craved for more. I knew that seeking revenge was the only satisfaction my heart craved for.

Several days passed, and I didn't get to do what I had become very fond of. Longing for it, I decided to try out other ways.

I learned about a drug lord, Rudolph, from someone in my friend circle. He was known to be a dangerous man and was even involved in supplying various harmful sorts of drugs to the people of my neighborhood.

Instantly, I knew what I had to do. After getting his address, I went to meet him. He lived somewhere very far away, in an old broken building.

I reached there and waited for my appointment. After a while, I was summoned to a room. I walked up there, entered the room, and saw Rudolph sitting in a comfortable chair behind a big desk in his full glory.

I walked up to the desk and stood there. He looked at me and said, "Sit down."

I sat on the chair and told him why I met with him.

I said, "I want to kill somebody and want money in return for it."

Listening to me, Rudolph's face lit up, and he smirked. He asked me, "Do you have a gun?"

I replied, "Yes."

He said to me, "I need you to take someone down for me. Make sure he is dead. All I want from you… is his head!"

I was taken aback by what he said and how he said it. I stared at him in shock, confused about whether I wanted to do it or not.

To be honest, I wanted to agree to it at once, but somewhere deep down, I was skeptical about it.

However, undecided, I replied, "I have to think about it."

Our meeting ended, and I came back home. On the way back, I kept thinking about what to do. I contemplated it and finally reached a conclusion.

Yes, I want to do it! I thought to myself. And all of this was while the police were still out looking for the murderer. ME! They were still unable to catch the culprit… and here I was, planning my second crime.

"That's fun!" I smirked while talking to myself.

A couple of days had passed since my meeting with Rudolph. I still had his contact number, so I gave him a call.

After a few rings, he picked up. I said, "Hey, this is Randy. We talked about the job the other day."

I heard him laughing from the other end of the line. With a touch of evil in his laughter, he said, "I knew you would make the right move. Working for me is the best thing you will ever have to do!"

When I heard him accepting my proposal, I was delighted. I was employed full-time, and I was very excited. And, after all, that was what I liked to do.

I asked him, "When do I start?"

Rudolph replied, "Whenever you like. Just deliver the head to me. But before that, come meet me."

I went to meet him. We sat down in his office, and he offered me some wine. Along with that, he discussed the plan with me.

He gave me a map explaining the plan I was supposed to carry out. It was a list of ten people who didn't pay him his money back. Furthermore, he asked me to take down two people in the same week.

I didn't know why these people on the list took money from him, nor did I know the severity of the situation. And I didn't pay much attention to it either. I just focused on the good part; I finally got a job, and the work seemed consistent.

By the end of the meeting, I asked him, "How much will you pay me?"

Rudolph replied, "Let's not discuss this right now. I will give you a surprise."

I have never been fond of surprises, so I insisted on immediate full disclosure.

"OK. It's going to be $50,000. I'll throw in an extra five grand if you deliver the head to me by tomorrow. Make sure he's dead!"

When I heard the amount, my jaw dropped. I was happy, surprised, and confused at the same time. I was overwhelmed with emotions and couldn't figure out what to reply.

The meeting ended, and I came home. I had not heard a word from Jason in a while, but I wanted to hear from him.

I reached my house, went inside and sat on my bed in my bedroom. The house was dark inside, and there was absolute silence. I put the plan and the map inside my cupboard safely.

I called Jason, but he didn't answer. I kept saying his name repeatedly, and then, I finally heard a word from him.

He replied inside my head as I lay down in my bed.

He was happy! In an instant, he cleared all my confusion. He was delighted that I got a good deal of money in return for doing something I would enjoy.

His assuring voice reverberated in my thoughts, "Get done with it tonight!"

I was so happy I could do so much with such a huge amount of money. And I knew that this was just the first target. After that, many more awaited me.

Shortly after, I fell asleep peacefully and was enthralled by what the coming day had to offer me.

The first thing I did the next morning was to take out the plan Rudolph had provided me. I thoroughly read it and figured out all the details of my first target.

Jackson was my first target. I didn't know the reason why Rudolph wanted him dead, but I had to do it anyway.

I knew his name and his address, but I didn't know much about his personal life. I wondered if he was married, had kids, or had any pets.

I freshened up, changed, and quickly had a bite. I took my car to take a tour around the place. Recci. I pulled up near his house. It was a pretty hot and humid spring day.

I moved closer to his house and found him sitting shirtless in his yard. He had a baby in his lap, and a couple of children played in the yard. He watched the children play while smoking a cigarette.

I looked at him from far away so he couldn't see me. I wondered if he was a good father. I wondered where his wife would be. I was preoccupied by the thoughts of what would happen to his family if I killed him.

I sat in the car and drove back. While Jason was shocked about what I had done, I kept driving.

Jason's voice echoed in my head, "Are you kidding me?"

However, I knew what I was doing. I loved kids and didn't want to cause them any distress.

How Jackson sat in his yard with his kids reminded me so much of my uncle. I kept thinking to myself that I couldn't do it. I couldn't do this to the kids!

I reached out to Jackson as soon as I reached home. I couldn't find almost anything fishy about him. I was so confused as to why Rudolph wanted me to kill him if he didn't have anything against him.

Jackson had a clean record. There were no charges or arrest warrants against him. I was so confused and spent the whole day distracted by the situation.

Soon, it was time for bed. I slept quite uncomfortably that night. The same thing had consumed my mind, making me unable to sleep peacefully.

I really wanted to kill him for the $50,000, but I couldn't figure out the reason for it. I craved to take revenge on somebody, but without a particular reason, I just couldn't do it.

The next day, I woke up feeling agitated. Suddenly, I heard Jason say, "Look what you did, Randy! You let go of $55,000. You are such a fool. Go get this job done!"

Jason said exactly what I wanted to hear. It wasn't long until he convinced me again. I thought, *Yes, Jason, I don't care. You're right. I will do it!*

This time, I decided to borrow my friend's car. Before that, I gathered my mask and my gun from the cupboard. Feeling enthusiastic, I looked at my gun with a smile on my face.

I put the gun inside my jacket. Until then, my friend had dropped his car off at my place. I told him I had a doctor's appointment and my car had broken down. I got into the car and pulled up in Jackson's block. As I walked to his house, I was consumed with self-disgust. At the bottom of my heart, I didn't want to kill him without any reason. But I also wanted the money, so I had to do it today, no matter what!

Jackson was in the yard, so I stopped at a distance. The next moment, I saw his wife coming out in the yard. She looked grieved and unhappy. I wondered what happened and looked at her carefully.

What happened next enraged me to my core and provided me a reason to kill Jackosn as soon as possible.

As she came out of the door, he ran to her and started beating her. He beat her mercilessly in the yard until she started crying and begging him to stop.

I was shaken. He beat her… the mother of his kids. But why would he do that? Even if there would be a reason, he shouldn't have beat her heartlessly.

Now, I was keen on killing him and planned to return at night and do what must be done!

I went back home and waited impatiently for the night. When the clock ticked 9:00 pm, I left the house and was on the road.

I reached Jackson's house and parked my car at a little distance. I walked up to his house and rang the doorbell. Within a minute, his wife opened the door. My heart sank as I saw her. I pitied her and wanted to take vengeance on Jackson on her behalf.

I had a mask on and asked her where he was. She replied, "He is not home. He has gone to the bar. You can meet him there."

I went to the Cool Night Bar just around the corner. I parked my car nearby in a dark spot to avoid being seen. He took a while to come out of the bar—I had to wait three hours before I saw him coming out with a couple of his friends.

They were drunk and weren't able to walk properly. They walked home from the bar, and I followed them in my car, maintaining my distance.

As I followed them, I knew that he had never hurt me or done anything else to me. But I wanted to do it for his wife. I wanted to take revenge on her behalf. A man who beats a woman doesn't deserve to stay alive.

I said to myself, "He will pay for what he did!"

I followed him up to the street where he lived. He was walking alone to his house, and I thought I would run him over, but no, I didn't do it. I desired to kill him face to face instead of from behind the back. That would have been cowardly, and I wasn't a coward.

I stopped the car, and in the next moment, I was on my feet. I called his name as I followed him, but he didn't answer. It was completely dark, and no one was around. I continued following him until he listened and turned around.

As he turned around, I said, "Look at me, at my face, before you die."

He seemed confused and was unable to comprehend what was happening. The next moment, I whipped my gun out and aimed at him.

He had a look of horror in his eyes. Before he could get a chance to run away, I pulled the trigger and shot him two times in his chest.

He dropped on the floor with his legs and hands straight and blood dripping out of his chest.

I looked at him mercilessly, and the memory of him beating his wife played at the back of my mind. I wasn't satisfied enough by just shooting him in the chest.

With that thought, I took a step forward and aimed at him again. This time, I shot him in the middle of his skull. He lay there on the floor, with his eyes wide open and blood flowing down his cheeks.

After that, I took out the machete from the car and beheaded him. There was blood all around, and Jackson was lying dead on the floor in a pool of his own blood.

I took out a box from the trunk of my car and put his head in it. I felt satisfied, as if a big chunk was taken off my chest... I felt relieved. The overwhelming emotions I felt earlier were nowhere to be found. I wasn't confused or sad anymore. I was happy that I did it!

Before leaving the crime scene, I put the box with Jackon's head inside the trunk and left him lying on the street, headless!

I wasn't scared of the consequences. I wasn't afraid that I might get caught by the police.

I drove to my house. Meanwhile, I called Rudolph to share the good news, but he didn't answer. I called him around five times, but when he didn't answer his phone, I decided to go to his place.

I reached there and rang the doorbell. One of his friends answered the door and took me to his office.

As he watched me enter his office, he asked, "Is it done?"

I replied, "Yes. Have a look in the box."

He looked at the box from afar and laughed like a heartless freak.

He was very happy and appreciated me a lot.

"Bravo! Very good!" He said.

He handed me an envelope with a reward for me. I took it and opened it to check the amount.

To my surprise, it was $60,000 instead of $55,000.

I was delighted to look at the amount and felt ecstatic. He rewarded me with *another* extra $5000.

At that moment, I felt like a great fit for this job. People couldn't earn in a year what I earned in a day.

I took the envelope, bowed to Rudolph, and left his office. I drove back to my home, feeling very excited. I reached, took a shower, and laid to rest.

In that while, I wanted to talk to Jason, but he wasn't there. I was exhausted and fell asleep as soon as my head hit the pillow.

The next morning, I woke up to Jason's voice.

"There he is," I said to myself.

Jason was happier than me. He praised me and said, "This is all we have ever wanted."

I said, "No, Jason. This is just the beginning!"

I had accepted the role of a full-time contract killer. I looked forward to committing more murders and earning surplus money from it.

Jason and I laughed, looking at the envelope full of money.

Chapter 5: The Joy of Killing

The vile and rude behavior I faced as I grew up turned me into a monster. The monster I had never thought I would become. I had never imagined being a monster before I moved to America.

The new passion I discovered captivated me to my very core. Never in my life had I thought that I possessed such a liking for it.

Realizing that killing people mercilessly was a newfound devotion for me. It had a strange and different sense of satisfaction. I was never conscious that something vicious like that could bring me profound pleasure. But here I was, standing among the glory of my new passion—*killing*.

I took pleasure in ending lives and inflicting pain upon others through acts of torture. It became my preference, and I treasured it for a reason.

The hate and resentment in my heart took a different form and became eminent. It became an unavoidable trait of my personality. Eventually, it became a part of my being!

Adding to my joy and contentment, getting paid heavily became another strong driving force. The superabundant money that Rudolph offered me was the cherry on top. The reward for it was surreal, and it overjoyed me. From my perspective, I could've even done it without even expecting a penny.

Standing at the window of my room, contemplating, I kept repeating in my head how much I loved to kill and torture people.

Even if I had to do it for free, I would have done it for the sake of my passion and my anger.

In moments like these, I talked to Jason, "I feel joy from doing what I am doing." With an evil smile on my face, my heart and brain were filled with loathing and abhorrence for the people I disliked. Even for the slightest and pettiest of reasons, I would kill them.

"We are being paid for it," Jason echoed in my mind.

Resonating with him completely and overjoyed to the extent that it was evident from my face, I instantly said with a smirk and a gleam in my eyes, "Yes, we are being paid heavily. We are getting a huge sum of money for doing what we love!"

One thing that stood out for me was the amount of money. With just one kill, I had already earned enough that I didn't have to work for the rest of my life. But my greed and hunger for money escalated with that note.

Apart from that, Jason was there with me. He stood by my side whenever I needed someone. In my times of pain, agony, and grief, he was the only one whom I could rely on.

Being my confidant, I shared everything with him that cooked inside my head. He was my mentor, life partner, and best friend. I did not fear judgment, even when I shared my deepest and darkest secrets with him.

Expressing my emotions to Jason was liberating. Being the only one to know my secrets, Jason thoroughly knew how I enjoyed my new passion. Besides that, he always supported me in doing what I loved and never discouraged me. I had come this far because of his consistent support and encouragement.

After analyzing myself, I knew there was no going back for me. I didn't want to return to normal. This was the new normal for me.

"Nothing could change me from what I have turned into. Nothing could distract me from being who I was," I murmured.

Being by my side as always, Jason encouraged me once more, "Yes!"

Jason always motivated me and boosted my spirits. He always left me with a sense of satisfaction and relief.

After my second murder, the police investigation began. However, I was completely unbothered by it because I was sure and extremely confident that I had left no clues behind.

My mind worked like a mastermind and made sure to carry out the murder smoothly and leave no fingerprints or traces that would lead them to me.

The police weren't able to get any leads for the recent murder or the first one I did. This gave me confidence, motivating me to do more.

I walked into my TV hall and turned on the television. Instantly, I had a sense of pride built within myself as I watched the news of the second murder I committed surfacing over the news channel.

The news of the person who was shot multiple times and brutally beheaded was all over the television. I took a glance, quickly skipping onto one channel from the other.

Sitting in front of the TV and being lost in my thoughts, the sound of the news being played in the background echoed in my ears. Occupied by my thoughts, I felt proud of myself. Glorifying my confidence and my skills, I craved to attempt more.

Distracting from my thoughts and observations, I shifted my focus to the channel. The news said that the police were still unable to identify the beheaded dead body.

In my subconscious, I was sure that they wouldn't be able to catch me. With an evil laughter, I said, "That's none of my business. I am just here to watch the news and enjoy."

I laughed at them, realizing they were trying so hard, but they couldn't catch me. With an intense gaze on the television, I murmured to myself with an evil grin, "After all, I didn't do it… or maybe I did!"

The day passed by with a blink of an eye. Now anticipating the next day even more, I went to bed and dozed off in a minute. The self-satisfaction and pride made me sleep so peacefully like I had never slept before.

After waking up the next day, I thought I would call Rudolph at 11:00, so I carried out all my daily tasks until it was time.

Soon, the clock ticked 11:00, and I picked up the phone. I dialed his number, and it rang a couple of times before he picked up.

As he picked up, I greeted him, "Hey man, how are you? Can I meet you?"

I knew Rudolph didn't like to discuss anything over the phone; rather, he wanted to meet in person. I asked him for a meeting.

Agreeing to it without any concerns or questions, he asked me to meet at 4:00 pm.

Shortly after, it was 4:00 pm already when I left my house to meet him. Within a few minutes, I arrived at his house and went inside. There, he sat in his office, looking at me with a hawk-like gaze and a smile on his face. Maybe he knew why I was there to meet him.

I approached him and sat down. The next thing I said to him was, "When do you want this second guy to go? When do you want me to take him down? You gave me a list of ten guys, and nine are still left."

Rudolph looked at me closely. He liked the passion I carried. He was impressed by the determination and motivation I had for the job I did.

He replied, "Sooner is better."

As I heard him say that, my heart jumped with excitement. Thinking that, finally, I would be doing another task that I loved, I felt exhilarated.

Rudolph asked me, "Did you burn down the list and the plan I gave you?"

I had gotten rid of the list already, so I nodded.

He nodded in agreement and continued, "This time, I will reward you even better."

I knew that he cared for me and wasn't a miser either. Initially, I was easily lured with money, but this time, I had some other intentions.

I wanted to do it for self-satisfaction and not reward. While money was a plus, the main reason I had now was the power I felt when I committed a murder. I sought gratification more than the money.

Having faith and trust in Rudolph, I didn't ask for an advance payment and agreed on the deal without showing any concerns.

The meeting ended quickly after that, and I returned home looking forward to my third murder.

I sat in solace, pondering over the situation. It baffled me how the dynamics changed for me. The power and satisfaction I felt after killing and torturing someone amazed me. I wasn't even scared a tiny bit; instead, I felt extremely confident after every murder. Moreover, the control I felt after taking a life was inexplicable.

The realization stuck with me that it was just the start, and there was so much more to come my way. I looked forward to it eagerly. The anticipation and excitement were astonishing, and I was ready for it!

Chapter 6: Lessons Learned In Blood

I rested in my bed, looking up at the ceiling and preoccupied with my thoughts. I was thinking about my third murder. How was I going to do it?

I knew what I was going to do with my third target and had decided to behead him, too. The thought of it didn't bother me at all, and I was okay with it. I was looking forward to it.

Apart from that, I was overjoyed with the money. I had never seen this much money before and couldn't believe it was all mine.

As I lay on my bed, excited about the money and my third murder, I desperately waited for Jason. I sought his validation, but he was nowhere to be found. However, I slept peacefully that night. I woke up the next day in a pool of money.

Oh my... the thrill and excitement I felt couldn't be expressed in words.

The first thing I did was to get a brand-new Infiniti for myself. I rushed to the store as soon as I finished breakfast. I reached the showroom with my pockets full of money.

The dealer showed me around, suggesting various new cars, but I wanted the black Infiniti.

I spotted the one I liked the most. It stood out in a corner with its polished exterior, emitting an aura of luxury and refinement. The sleek contours and shining finishes captivated my attention, while the interior boasted premium materials and cutting-edge technology. It embodied sophistication and elegance, which I was looking for.

The moment I looked at it, I was in love and decided to get it right then.

Pointing at the car, I told the dealer, "That's it, that's what I want."

He looked at me for a brief second and quoted me the price.

"It is for $44,950, sir."

"That's alright. Get it for me," I responded

Instantly, I whipped out heaps of cash from my pocket.

His jaw dropped to the floor with his mouth wide open. Surprised, The dealer asked me, "Woah, where did you get all his money from?"

I was pissed to hear that. What did he mean by that question?

I said coldly, "You don't need to worry about that. Show me the car, or I will go somewhere else."

Instantly, the salesman apologized for his stupid remark. He guided me to the car to take a closer look.

I looked at him with no fear and a smirk on my face. I examined the car, and everything seemed fine to me. Finally reaching the billing counter, I purchased the car of my dreams.

The car was taken out of the showroom so I could drive it home. I sat in the beauty and hit the accelerator.

The gush of wind hit my face as I rolled down the window.

But then, someone whispered in my ear as I drove, "What have you done? The money you have in your pocket, every single bill, is blood money. Are you happy with that?"

"What was that?" I thought.

It wasn't Jason, and I was taken aback for a second. I was sure that Jason wouldn't say something like that to me. I wondered who it was.

Maybe it was God's voice, or maybe I was losing my mind.

However, I ignored it and continued to drive.

I reached home and parked my new car in the garage. I went inside my house and went straight to the kitchen.

Grabbing a bottle of water from the fridge, I gulped it as quickly as possible. Man... I was thirsty!

I went back to think about my third target again. And thought, why not get it done today, and that too in my new car.

As soon as I made up my mind, I felt thrilled.

I freshened up myself and left the house. As I had already done my homework on this guy, I knew where to go.

His name was George, and he lived far from my house.

I drove for about 15 minutes before I reached my destination. I drove around the vicinity, searching for his residence, before I finally spotted his house.

I parked a few blocks away from his house. I wore a hoodie that covered almost my entire face so nobody could recognize me. I also had my mask in case I needed to wear it.

Walking down the street, I reached his door and rang the doorbell. Before that, I put my mask on in a way that half of my face was covered.

I waited there impatiently, waiting for him to open the door so that I could kill him immediately without wasting a single minute. The front yard was empty, and it was pin-drop silence. I started to become angry and impatient. I just wanted to get it over with, but he was making it difficult for me.

Quite a few minutes passed by, and nobody opened the door. I was furious. I walked away from the door and roamed around the block for a while. Again, I came back and rang the doorbell once again. Much to my disappointment, no one answered this time too.

Exasperation had taken over me, and I wanted to kill George as soon as possible. I put my finger on the doorbell, exerting full force on it. I rang it for five straight seconds, sure someone would open it this time.

A few minutes passed, and no one answered yet.

"Damn!"

I was enraged.

I walked away from the house and went to sit in my car. I sat in the car for ten minutes to calm myself down and compose myself. I decided to try it for the last time.

Once again, I gathered my courage and marched to George's house. Without wasting any second, I rang the bell and stood there, trying to keep my calm.

Deep down in my heart, I wanted to behead George the moment he opened the door because he made me wait for so long.

I was getting very impatient when the door creaked open. To my surprise, it wasn't George but a little kid standing before me, and his eyes fixed at mine.

Damn! Why? Why it has to be the family? I exclaimed inside my head.

I looked at the kid and didn't say a word for a brief while. He was around ten. His face was filled with innocence, and his eyes glistened.

"Hey, little one. Is George home?" I asked him.

"Daddy is sleeping," the kid replied. "What is your name?"

"My name is Thomas. Tell him that I stopped by."

He looked at me and asked another question.

"How do you know my father?"

Before answering him, I contemplated what to reply.

"We used to be friends. We used to hang out. I haven't seen him in years."

"Do you want me to wake him up?" The kid asked.

"No, buddy, it is okay. I will come back later."

After that, I left. Thank God he didn't wake George up, else I would have to kill him in front of his kid, and that would be devastating for the kid.

I spotted a tricycle and various toys when I walked past the front yard. That made me think he had several kids.

Children always make it difficult for me to do the task with ease.

I reached my car and drove away. As I left the area, I felt disappointed that I wasn't able to kill George. I wished to do it as soon as possible and present his head to Rudolph.

I reached home and went to bed.

The next day, I woke up determined to kill George that day. I waited for the day to turn into night.

As soon as the clock hit 8 pm, I left my house with my gun, my mask, and my machete. I put everything in the car and drove to his house.

I reached his block and circled his house for a while in my car. He was there, out in his yard and preparing to go somewhere. As I drove past his house, he made eye contact with me. I stared at him in a hawk-like manner. But he couldn't recognize me because of the face mask I was wearing.

He started walking, and I followed him in my car. As I reached near to him, I called him out.

"Hey."

He stopped and turned around upon hearing my voice. He looked tough and also lost in his own world. It felt like something was up with him. He had a hoodie on and smoked a cigar.

I walked out of my car and went near him, meanwhile wondering what he had done to Rudolph.

"Hi. What is up, man?" He asked.

As a new Black guy in the neighborhood, I tried to get to know him. I tried to make a small talk with him.

"Do you live around here?" I asked.

I was talking to the man who was going to be the victim number three in just a few seconds.

"Yes, I live just right there," he said, pointing toward his residence.

"Do you know anyone who sells *dog food* here?" I asked him.

"Dog food?" He seemed perplexed.

I thought he would be a street guy, but he didn't know what I was talking about.

"I mean drugs."

"Oh, I have them. I sell drugs. What do you want?" He replied instantly.

"I am looking for some good stuff."

"What do you use?"

"I use cocaine and sometimes crack, too, but I hate marijuana," I replied.

With a burst of laughter, he said, " Are you kidding me?"

"No, I am serious," I said.

We had a conversation like that for a few minutes. I pulled out 200 dollars from my pocket and offered it to him.

As he looked at the money, he pulled out a crack bag from the pocket of his hoodie.

I got a reason to kill George. Drugs!

We walked to a lone alley before he handed it over to me. It was dark and deserted. I smiled inside as he led me to the spot where he would get himself killed.

We walked down and stopped in the corner. He handed the crack to me and said, "I am giving some extra crack to you. Take my number and call me if you need anything again."

I thanked him and said goodbye with a fist bump.

He started to walk in front of me, and I strolled behind him.

As he reached a few steps ahead of me, I stopped at my spot and called out his name,

"George!"

He stopped immediately and turned around. He looked confused.

"How do you know my name?" He had a hint of nervousness in his tone.

"Because I am here for you," I replied with a deepened voice.

"What do you mean? What do you want from me?" He asked me nervously.

"I need the truth, George. What does Rudolph want from you? Tell me the truth, and I will let you live."

I guess he didn't take me seriously and looked me in the eye, "What do you mean? I don't get it."

The next moment, I pulled out my gun and aimed at him.

He was surprised, and his face flushed with horror.

"Tell me the truth. I am giving you the last chance to speak. How much do you owe Rudolph?" I said sternly.

As he looked at the gun, he went down to his knees and begged for his life.

"Please let me go," he cried.

"Tell me, how much money do you owe him?" I yelled.

He replied instantly, "I owe him $500,000."

I was surprised to hear such a big amount. That was a lot!

I asked him the reason. He replied, "I took it for drugs."

"I will give you $200,000 cash. Please let me go."

He offered me money so I wouldn't kill him, but it wasn't way more than what Rudolph had promised me. Also, I was loyal to my boss and had no intentions of betraying him.

"You are going to pay for it," I said furiously.

I wasn't going to have mercy on him. he cried in front of me for his life, but my heart didn't melt.

I aimed at his forehead and shot him from a 10 feet distance. I had no fear as I pulled the trigger and shot him without giving it a second thought. He fell on the street, and blood splashed out.

I stood there, looking at him mercilessly. I was proud of myself for committing my third murder. I saw him bleed, his eyes shut and, and his mouth slightly open.

I picked out the machete from the car and proceeded to cut his head off. I beheaded him, drops of blood splashing around as I separated his head from his body.

I picked out a bag from the car and put the head inside it. I placed the bag in the trunk of my car and threw my mask along the way.

I glanced at George for the last time, lying on the street without his head. Nobody would be able to recognize him.

I was numb and didn't feel anything anymore. I sat in my car and drove away, leaving his body on the street just like that.

I arrived directly at Rudolph's residence to drop off the parcel to him—George's head. I was all alone, driving to meet Rudolph. I wished to talk to Jason, but he was nowhere to be found.

Rudolph was waiting for me in his office. He couldn't contain his excitement when I handed over him the parcel.

"Did he mention anything to you?" Rudolph asked.

"No. But, I am curious how much he owed you?" I asked.

"Millions of dollars!" He said.

He was very satisfied with my work and handed me an envelope full of money. I accepted the reward, and to my astonishment, I didn't feel content after receiving the cash this time. I felt emotionless and didn't turn back because I had nothing to do with the head anymore.

Randolph summoned me back and asked, "What happened? Are you getting weak on me?"

"No, I am just having a bad day."

"Well, this will make you feel better," he pointed toward the $100,000 he had paid me.

The cash was crisp and fresh. It smelt like it just came out of a machine.

At that moment, I heard Jason laughing. I couldn't figure out why, as I couldn't comprehend any emotions.

Shaking Randolph's hand, I could only see him smiling. I didn't say a word. He mentioned the remaining guys whom I had to kill. I uttered nothing and left after Rudolph was done talking.

I drove away and reached my house feeling lost.

I dropped on the couch and gazed at the ceiling. I wasn't sure why I was feeling that way.

No signs of anger, resentment, or evil were present in me. Even the money didn't make me feel happy.

I was shocked at what was happening to me. Maybe I was scared for my future. Maybe I was terrified of where I was heading.

I had become heartless, and those feelings of uncertainty shook me. This was not how I felt a few days ago.

I invoked myself to think the other way. I forced myself to believe in my powers. I knew how confident I was and had mastered the art of killing.

The sense of invincibility I had in me was triggered again. I was uncertain, but it hadn't vanished completely. Maybe it was a hint for me to stop what I was doing or a lesson for me to learn.

Sitting on the couch, contemplating, I realized that it was almost midnight.

I was exhausted and wanted to rest. Thus, I went to my room, freshened up, and went to bed. Lost in my thoughts, I didn't realize when I dozed off.

Chapter 7: Seeking Redemption

It happened for the first time that I felt a strange and unfamiliar restlessness. Never have I ever felt like that before or after murdering somebody. Even Jason wasn't with me this time, and I hadn't heard from him for quite some time.

The next day, I woke up with a heavy heart. I felt heavy and burdened, and I couldn't figure out why. After all, what I had been doing was the thing I had come to love the most. The joy and fulfillment I experienced from torturing people, followed by brutally murdering them, was profound. But now, I couldn't figure out what was happening to me.

My thoughts and contemplation kept me busy the whole. I spent the whole day thinking about what I had been doing or if I wanted to continue doing it. I wasn't sure, and I couldn't decide anything.

However, the day went by, and I looked forward to the next day as Rudolph had already given me two new targets. Deep down, I didn't want to go hunt them, but I was compelled to because I had promised my boss—Rudolph.

I waited for the next evening to look for Henry and Jeff, the new targets.

My first target was Henry. Rudolph had told me everything about him. I knew where he lived and reached his house instantly. I noticed that the front door of his residence was open, so I stomped in without hesitation. As soon as I entered, I observed that he had a family, two kids around three and four years old, and a beautiful wife.

Damn! I was shocked and frustrated to see his family. I didn't like hurting people's families for no obvious reason, but I couldn't do anything. It wasn't in my control anymore. My circumstances forced me to do it anyway. No matter how hard I tried, I couldn't prevent myself from doing something unacceptable.

However, a corner in my heart was still present, which remained unbothered by everything. The cruel and savage nook provided me the strength to carry out something extremely brutal and ruthless yet again.

To intimidate Henry, I did something barbaric. My cruel instinct made me kill his wife.

The darkness I had gathered inside me made me take out my gun, aim at her forehead, and pull the trigger. Within a second, she was on the floor, lying in her own pool of blood.

Henry and his children stood in horror, trying to comprehend what happened.

After that, I walked toward him and grabbed him from the back so that he couldn't move. Pushing him on the floor, I grabbed a piece of rope and tied his hands from the back. Grabbing him forcefully, I pulled him up and dragged him out. His kids were terrified, crying hysterically. I didn't stop for a second and left them there, standing in despair—their mother lying dead on the floor and their father being dragged out of the house. For a second, I thought about what would happen to the kids after I left, but I managed to leave the house in the heat of the moment.

Henry was alive. I didn't kill him and just delivered him to Rudolph. He would do anything he wanted to, I thought to myself. Meanwhile, I wondered how much Henry owed to Rudolph.

I delivered my target, Henry, to Rudolph as quickly as possible. I wasn't concerned about the money anymore and didn't even wait to receive the cash; I left Rudolph's house immediately.

This time, it was different, and I didn't know why. Something was wrong with me. Maybe I didn't realize it, but deep inside my heart, something had changed. I didn't long for any type of reward or appreciation. I just wanted to get done with it.

Contrary to that, it was entirely different previously. I used to look forward to appreciation from my boss. His complimentary words would make my heart full and overjoyed. The money I received in return for the task excited me. But now, I didn't feel any of those; it was just a numbing feeling in my heart; my mind was lost somewhere with no signs of contentment.

I reached my house. It was silent and dark inside, just like my heart and soul. I walked toward the refrigerator and took a water bottle as I entered the house. I sat on the couch in the same darkness, with no lights on. The moonlight entered through the window as I sipped water while sitting alone on the couch. The feeling of loneliness swamped me. I was alone and had nobody to talk to, not even Jason. I wondered where he was, leaving me all alone by myself. It had never happened before that Jason wasn't there for me when I needed him. I couldn't do anything but wait for him to talk to me because I wanted to share my feelings with somebody, and I had no one. I was utterly alone!

Filled with despair, I got up from the couch and walked to my room. Without even eating anything, I went to bed. I already had a task for the next day. No matter if I wasn't in the state of doing it, I had no choice but to skip it because of my promises to Rudolph.

My next target was Jeff. Rudolph had given me all the necessary information to track him down. I looked at his picture and thought he might be someone I knew. I wondered what he had to do with Rudolph; maybe he was one of the hitmen for Rudolph, like me, or he owed him money as well.

I reached the vicinity where Jeff lived. Circling in my car around the streets, I looked for his house. I stopped at his house and waited for him to come out.

The door opened, and somebody stepped out of it. My heart jumped in triumph that I had found my target, but to my surprise, it wasn't him. An old lady walked out of the house along with her husband. I was bummed.

I got out of my car and went to the old couple, inquiring about Jeff. I told them that I was looking for my long-lost friend. I was told that he had left the house several weeks ago.

I was alarmed. Jeff was one wicked man. He had changed his residence, but Rudolph didn't know about it. He probably knew that he was on the hit list.

However, I left to look around for him, feeling he might be nearby. I drove around one block to another, looking into every nook and corner. My eyes searched for him like a surveillance camera. A couple of hours passed before I stopped at the corner of the street. A small department store was at the corner, just below an old building. The store door opened, and a middle-aged man walked out of it.

Jeff... it was Jeff! I recognized him from the photo. Finally, I got him and felt a sense of relief. I had decided I wouldn't kill him either, like Henry. I was only going to deliver him to Rudolph, and the rest will be taken care of by Rudolph himself.

I stopped for a brief while and planned how I was going to approach him. Meanwhile, he walked across the street and strolled forward. Until then, I knew what I had to do.

First, I followed him in my car for a few minutes, then parked it in a dark corner. The street was empty and completely dark, with no street lights. I got out of the car and followed him silently, without saying a word.

As he passed by a couple of buildings, I called him, "Hey, Jeff."

He stopped and turned around. We were facing each other now. It was so dark that it was almost impossible to recognize my face. I didn't have my mask on and just wore a sweater. I didn't even care if he recognized my face or not.

As he turned around, I pointed my gun at him. He was shocked and terrified. Horror was evident on his face, and he was scared to the extent that he couldn't even utter a single word.

Without saying a word or speaking to him, I walked closer to him and hit his head with the back of the gun. He was down on the floor. I kicked him multiple times and punched his gut. I beat him up like an animal; he bled through his head and lay almost dead on the street, but he was still breathing. Then, I grabbed him up and threw him in the trunk of my car. I drove as fast as I could and dropped him off to Rudolph.

From all the beating and hitting, I felt angry and frustrated. Previously, I had forgotten to collect the due amount for Henry's head. I walked into Rudolph's office and found him waiting for me with an envelope full of cash. It was $200,000, an amount that I had never even seen before. That was a lot of money for me. I should have been extremely excited and overjoyed, but that was not the case. I felt no emotions, excitement, happiness, or even a hint of joy.

I left with the envelope and drove back to my house. I was lost in my thoughts and wondered why I felt unhappy. The money didn't mean anything to me now; it felt surreal before. The news of my murders being cast over the channels still didn't bother me. I was not scared, but I felt dead inside, devoid of any sensations or feelings.

I looked for answers but couldn't manage to find any. I called Jason and didn't get a response from him either. I was worried about where he had gone as I wanted to talk to him. I needed someone to share my intrusive and unsettling thoughts. I wanted to explain the strange emptiness inside my heart to somebody, but I had no one to talk to. The loneliness haunted me, and I wanted to run away. Unfortunately, I didn't have many options for myself.

I pondered why I felt this way and realized I might need professional help. The loneliness was cutting deep inside my heart, and I couldn't bear it anymore.

Therefore, I finally decided to reach out for help and ended up calling a psychiatrist. To my dismay, they had no appointments until next month. I didn't lose hope and called another clinic, but they had no slots for me until a few months later. Keeping my hopes high, I reached out to another and was told that they, too, were fully booked. Some of them didn't even accept my insurance.

I was frustrated and would have smacked them if I had visited in person. Thankfully, I had only called to make an appointment.

Nearly every mental professional I knew was completely booked and had no slots left for me. Disappointment and hopelessness swamped me, resulting in frustration and anger.

I was exasperated, and resentment took over me. I was disgusted that every professional was booked and didn't have time for me when they were supposed to help people like me.

Moreover, I was also nervous that somebody would find out about the money I had. I didn't want to tell anyone about it and get into any form of trouble because I didn't have a legitimate job.

I wondered if I had somebody to talk to other than a therapist, but unfortunately, no one could help me. Even Jason didn't come to my rescue this time. I was left in despair and sorrow, a deserted feeling and unfamiliar emptiness.

My mental health had been compromised after everything that had happened over time. It didn't start deteriorating when I began to kill or torture people. Instead, it was since I moved to the States and faced discrimination so often, which led to anger and resentment building up inside me. I never paid much attention to it before, but it was there… lurking at the back of my mind. Now, it was emerging in such a way that I had never even thought about.

The joy and exhilaration that came from murdering people was rather short-lived; it didn't last long. I realized that I needed help as soon as possible because the mental state I was existing in was something very alarming. I should have been more aware of it, vigilant and observant. Nevertheless, I hoped that it wasn't too late.

Chapter 8: Embracing Darkness

I had been waiting desperately to get an appointment with a good therapist, but everyone was booked. Some were booked for four months, some for five months, and some were unavailable until eight months.

I was trying to overcome the guilt I was drowning in. I was lost, searching for Jason, but no one was there for me. I sat on the couch, occupied by my thoughts.

What have I done? Is this what I wanted to do? I thought to myself.

I had come to the conclusion that that there was no way out now. I was trapped and had no other option but to make my way out of the darkness. However, I believed it was time to embrace the darkness and accept my fate.

Rejecting all the theories of remorse, redemption, and repentance in my mind, I decided to step forward with what I had been doing.

Rudolph had already assigned me another target. It was another guy from the list of ten people I had to kill. I had already killed many of them; now, just a few were left.

There, I decided to get done with it. I accepted it was my fate and that I could do nothing to stop it.

The guy I had to kill was one of the top drug dealers and owed a considerable sum of money to Rudolph. Earlier, Rudolph had already paid someone to kill him, but the attempt remained unsuccessful. I knew that it would be difficult to kill him. Thus, I had to be very careful and attentive.

His name was Jackson; I was determined to kill him now. I had all his details: his address, phone number, and picture. I knew how he looked, so I could easily recognize him.

It was late at night, about 9:00 pm, when I left to look out for him. It was already dark, and I could barely see anyone on the street.

I reached Jackson's address. He had a big house with six cars and two motorcycles in his garage. He must be rich, I assumed. I walked up to his door and rang the bell. Nobody answered. I patiently stood there, waiting for someone to answer, but no one answered the door. After waiting for a good 30 minutes, I headed back to home.

As I walked toward my car, I felt that this target would be difficult to kill, and now, more than ever, I just wanted to get rid of Jackson.

I reached home, opened the door, and went straight to my room. As I changed into my pajamas, I kept on thinking about him. I lay in my bed, thinking about Jackson's house, and his face kept roaming in my thoughts. While thinking about him, I went into deep slumber.

The following day, I woke up all pumped up to get the job done.

After finishing everything around the house, I left to stalk Jackson again. I reached his house and parked further away so nobody could see or recognize me. I saw Jackson coming out of his home.

He took one of his cars and sped away. I stalked him in my car, thinking about where he would go. He seemed in a hurry.

Slow down, man, I thought to myself while I followed him.

He drove to the nearby market and parked in front of a jewelry store. I parked close to him and waited for his next move.

I went behind him into the store and idly kept looking at different stuff. I made sure not to look suspicious. To pretend like a regular customer, I got a necklace for my daughter, which was approximately $200.

Meanwhile, I kept an eye on Jackson. I saw him choosing a diamond necklace for $20,000.

He must be filthy rich, I said in my head,

As we both crossed paths in the store, I said a little *Hi* with a subtle smile. He replied back with the same grace. He seemed like a nice guy to me. Little did he know that I was there to stalk him, and my ultimate goal was to murder him. I couldn't wait for the right time and spot to commit this crime. I was determined to kill him ruthlessly. There was no remorse left inside me. I just wanted to get done with it. I was not afraid of God. I wasn't terrified of the authorities; now. There was no possibility of redemption for me anymore.

I guess it was my final call to turn into a ruthless killer!

As I left the store, I headed to the parking lot, sat in my car, and left. I stopped at a distance and waited for Jackson's car to pass ahead of me.

As he took over, I followed him. All the way, I kept reminding myself that his time was over. He reached his house and pulled over in his garage. I stopped at a distance, almost three houses away from his home.

I noticed everybody in the neighborhood who saw him greeted him warmly. Including the elderly, adults, and kids, everyone knew him and extended their greetings. It seemed like he had a lot of respect in the neighborhood. Maybe he was a nice guy. Kind and respectful toward everybody.

I waited in my car for a while and left for home. That was it for the day. I decided to do a little more stalking the next day. So I could kill him confidently, without any suspicions or mistakes.

The next morning, I left my house in another car so nobody would notice me. I pulled close to his house and saw him coming out the door. He sat in the car and headed somewhere I didn't know. I followed him until he stopped in front of a hospital where his son was admitted, injured and badly wounded. I followed him into the hospital, walking up the stairs to the room where his son was. He was only around seven years old. I stopped in the waiting area and waited patiently for Jackson.

After a while, he walked out of the room. I decided to walk into the room to see his son. I lowered my cap on my face so that my face was covered and unrecognizable. As I entered, I saw his son raising his head from the pillow and asking, "Who is it?"

"Oops, sorry, wrong room."

I exited the room right away and walked into the waiting area. Jackson and I crossed paths. He didn't recognize me.

The walk to my car became a reality check session for me. I was skeptical now, whether to kill him or not. He was a father. He had a family. He had a wife. I had all these thoughts raging in my head, making me reassess my decision to kill him.

Somehow, I controlled my overthinking and reached home. I didn't do much throughout the day, instead of thinking about whether or not to kill Jackson.

The next day, I received a call from an unknown number. I became curious about who was calling me from a number that wasn't on my phone already. Therefore, I answered the call.

It was Rudolph. "Hello," he said.

"How is everything going so far?"

"Everything is going smooth," I replied, not asking anything else. I knew already who he was. I recognized the voice. Thus, I didn't ask any more questions.

"I hope everything is going well, and everything should be done by the end of the night."

As he said it, I kept quiet. I knew what he meant. Without saying much, I ended the call.

The whole day, I didn't plan anything to kill Jackson. Soon, the day turned into night, and it was already too late.

I could have gone out to kill Jackson, but I didn't. I was too lazy to do it that day. Therefore, I decided to go to bed.

The next day, it was a bright, sunny morning. I was up early, fresh and active. I had a good night's sleep and was well-rested. But I knew deep down in my heart that I would have to do it today.

"This is the day to get rid of Jackson," I murmured.

I knew how far I had come; there was no going back now. So, I decided to do it tonight.

I prepared my Glock, face mask, jacket, and all the gear I had. I patiently waited for the sun to set, and that was when I left my house in my car.

I parked near his house and waited for him to come out of the door anytime. It was already dark, and nobody could barely recognize me.

I saw him riding one of his bikes, and he rode away quickly. I followed him in my car, thinking to hit him from behind. But then, I realized it wouldn't be a good decision to do so.

What if I miss the hit, and he fled away? Then, I grabbed my Glock and thought to shoot him from the back. But I could miss the shot, so I cut that thought off.

I decided to speed and stopped my car in front of his bike. He took off his helmet and shouted, "You son of a bitch!"

He continued to yell and called me names. He came near my car window when I pulled down my mask.

"I recognize you!"

I didn't say anything and kept quiet. I moved out of my car and pointed my gun at him.

It was dark all around, and no one, not even an animal, was present on that street. I was in the clear to shoot him and knew nobody would witness this murder.

"You are gone!" I said and pulled the trigger.

He fell on the floor, blood dripping from his forehead; his eyes rolled, and he fell on his back. At first, I thought to cut off his head, but I didn't. I didn't want to do it. So, I took some pictures to show Rudolph as proof.

I picked up his dead body and threw it in the corner, in the bushes.

I fled from the scene in my car, throwing my facemask in a trash can far away from the crime scene.

I didn't feel anything after murdering Jackosn. I guess I had become used to what I had been doing for quite some time. I enjoyed staying in this dark place and accepted it with all my heart.

The next day, I went to Rudolph's house to present him the proof and receive my reward. As I entered his office, I showed him the pictures, and he extended a bag full of cash. I accepted it, nervously looking at it and trying to open it. As I opened it, I could smell the cash already. It was a lot of money. Piles and piles of cash were inside the bag!

After I collected the money, I thanked him and left his office. I counted the money after reaching home, and there was half a million dollars. That was what I needed, after all!

I was proud of myself. I got the job done and got paid heavily for it.

"Ah! What an amazing feeling!"

I had accepted my life was a deep, dark journey filled with blood, crimes, and lies. I enjoyed what I was doing. I looked for Jason, but he still wasn't responding to me. Despite that, I did it, and I was proud of myself.

Chapter 9: Reaching Out for Help

I stayed at home the whole week. I didn't know what got into me, but I had a void in my heart—a feeling of strangeness and loneliness. Desperation was creeping up on me, making me feel alienated in this society. I wanted to live in my solitude. I tried to avoid interacting with my family.

I failed no matter how hard I tried to accept my crimes or make peace with them. I thought I was all right with continuing all the criminal activities when I committed the last murder, but something didn't fit well with me. My brain was numb. I was lost. And on top of everything, Jason wasn't there anymore. I felt like sitting in a dark corner or running somewhere far away.

A week went by, just like that. I picked up my phone and saw at least ten missed calls from Rudolph. I knew what he would have to say. I decided to call him back; maybe that would ease me up.

I dialed his number and waited for him to answer. It was ringing, and I waited for him to pick it up. After a few seconds, I was just about to put down the phone when I heard him say, "Hey, man. Where were you lost? I thought you had run away."

"What do you want now?" I asked.

"Another target."

"Okay."

I had another task… one more murder. My mind echoed.

I wasn't sure if I should do it or not. I wanted it to end all the dirty stuff, but somewhere in my mind, I felt like committing another crime.

I was baffled, anxious, and unaware of what was actually wrong with me. I felt satisfied every time I killed someone, but later on, a feeling of regret or remorse took over me. I was unsure if the strange feelings were due to what I had already done or the anticipation of what I had to do next.

Another day went by just like that, confused and nervous. I also knew Rudolph wouldn't be quite happy about it if I didn't hit the last target.

"What the fuck is wrong with me!" I murmured.

I ignored all the feelings and went by my day. I decided to talk a way around the neighborhood. It was eight at night. The streets were empty, and it was pin-drop silent. I walked around for fifteen minutes to divert my mind.

As I walked past a street, it reminded me of one of the streets on which I committed my first murder. I got flashbacks of how I killed my first target, then the second, and so on.

I had flashbacks of my childhood and how I was bullied throughout when I moved here from Guyana, how I never felt welcomed here, and how I was discriminated against. Every memory of it was still fresh in my subconscious. Everything that happened over time was only because of my childhood traumas. Maybe it happened because I wanted to take revenge for all I had faced in childhood. I resented everyone and tried to take it out on people I thought deserved it. I liked punishing people, probably because I had been through heartbreak and despair.

Oh my! It boggled my mind. I had come to realize that I desperately needed help—professional help from a counselor. But, I was unable to get it because of the pathetic healthcare system in America. Nobody cared about us, and everyone just cared about money. I still had to wait for months to get a single appointment with a mental health professional.

I was done already and went back home. I wanted to sleep to calm myself down, but I couldn't sleep that night. I tried sleeping on every side of my body but couldn't. I wanted to shut my mind and stop thinking about my past and all that I had done. I got up and searched for sleeping pills nervously. I looked through all of the drawers but couldn't find any. Luckily, I found one when I reached the last drawer. I swallowed it instantly and waited for the medicine to kick in.

I didn't know when I dozed off.

I woke up the following day. I was tired. My mind was exhausted. Around 2 o'clock, my phone rang. I knew who it would be.

"What's up, man? When are you going to do it?" He asked straightly.

"I will think about it."

I didn't say anything else and ended the call.

I knew Rudolph wouldn't spare me. He would push me to do it; if I didn't, I might end up on a list that he would give to someone else. But I had to take my time to think about it.

The clock hit 08:00 when I decided to try it for the last time. My inner self was pushing me just to get done with it. Maybe it had become a habit that satisfied me, but it just didn't feel right after a while.

I took out the information Rudolph had given me about my new target. I took out my gear and went out to do some stalking.

I took my car and reached the spot where he lived. It was a little far away from where I lived, but I arrived without wasting time as it was already late, and there was almost no traffic on the roads.

I parked near his building and waited for the guy to come out. His name was Michael; he was a young man, maybe around 25 years old. I waited almost an hour for him.

After a while, I saw him coming out of his building. He was dressed casually and walked on the sidewalk quite casually.

He seems chill, I thought.

He walked down the road and stopped by at the corner in the dark. I saw him look around as if he wanted to ensure no one was looking. I leaned back into my seat, so I disappeared. A few minutes later, another young guy came running toward him. Both of them exchanged something and went on their way.

"Oh, drugs. I am gonna get him!" I murmured.

Both of them were so young and engaged in such activities. It agitated me. I decided to get rid of him then and there.

I went home and prepared myself for the next day. I prepared myself to complete the task at hand, but something in my subconscious wanted me to stop.

"Jason," I called, "I need you, buddy."

I got no reply. I sat there, pondering if I should do it or not. I was 50% inclined to do it, but the other 50% of me just wanted to stop all of this.

The night went by, and I woke up the following day with the thought of getting over him. I waited for the clock to hit 8:00 so I could leave for the last mission.

I had promised myself that it would be my last murder. I won't be doing anything like this after murdering Michael. I promised myself. I took my Glock and left the house.

I reached his building. I knew he would come again today to sell drugs.

I was right. He came out of the building at the same time as yesterday and went to the same corner. Today, a new guy came to get stuff from him. This guy was even younger than the one before.

I waited for them to get done with their business. As soon as Michael walked back to his house, I followed him.

He walked straight and turned left. It was a dark, silent street. I was going to kill him just here.

I walked out of my car and followed him.

"Michael," I called his name.

"Yeah. Do you want something?"

"Yes, I want to kill you."

He stood there for a second without any expressions and then laughed.

"Man, I just have some weed and opium right now. What do you…."

I shot him before he could even finish his sentence.

He fell on the floor, on his back, with a bullet in the middle of his forehead. Within a matter of seconds, he was lying in his own pool of blood.

I killed him without giving it a second thought, relentlessly. I was sure nobody saw me because there was no one around.

I picked up his body and put it in my car. But, I saw someone running fast at the corner of the street. I looked around but found no one. I ignored it and continued with my business.

I loaded him in my trunk and sped off.

When I reached home, I was not sure what I was going to do with his body. I thought for a brief while and decided to bury him in my backyard.

I dragged him to my backyard, picked up a shovel, and dug quickly. To be honest, I was nervous. I wanted nobody to see me. I had a strange fear about the person who saw me and got away. I wasn't sure if they saw me kill Michael or not.

Aside from worrying about that, I knew I needed to move fast and get rid of the body. I dug a ditch and buried Michael. It was 02:00 in the morning. Everybody was fast asleep.

After I finished it, I was out of breath, and sweat dripped down my face. I took a bottle of water out of the fridge and sat on the couch., trying to calm myself down. I chugged down the water and took deep breaths.

After a while, I felt a bit relaxed. I couldn't figure out why I was behaving that way. It hadn't happened before. That feeling was new to me.

Again, I was forced to think that I needed immediate help. I cursed the healthcare system once again, but I was helpless.

I just sat on the couch, and soon, I realized that it was dawn already.

Damn, I didn't sleep and kept sitting on the couch the whole time. I thought to myself.

I was lost. I was losing my mind. Something was incredibly wrong with me.

I wanted to say something to somebody, but I couldn't. Not even to my family or friends. Even Jason was lost somewhere. He had left me just like everyone else did in the past.

I was exhausted. My mind was churning.

"God! What is wrong with me," I murmured.

My phone rang. It was Rudolph.

"Are you done with the task?"

"Yes."

"Where is the proof?"

I realized that I had not collected any proof of the task I had completed. Damn!

"I have no proof. I dug him in my backyard."

"What? Have you gone nuts? I want proof, man. Otherwise, you won't have your reward."

He hung up.

I didn't want any reward anymore. I was over it already. I just wanted to get over everything that happened.

I was done!

I wasn't scared of Rudolph or didn't care about any consequences either.

I was numb, as if all the feelings inside me were dead!

Chapter 10: Facing Justice

The sun shone bright. I was still trying to process everything that had happened. I hadn't eaten or drank anything since last night. I hadn't even slept for a second.

I got up from the couch and entered the kitchen to get a glass of water. I fetched a bottle, poured myself a glass, and drank it. The first sip felt like I hadn't drank water in a while. My throat was dry like a desert. It quenched my thirst. I thought about eating something, but I wasn't hungry. I didn't feel like eating anything.

Feeling numb, I turned around to head to my room, and just then, I heard the doorbell ring.

"Who is it?" I murmured.

I walked toward the door and opened the door.

It was the police!

I was shocked. It felt like a punch in my stomach. My heart sank, my blood went cold, and my soul left my body.

What is happening? Am I going to get arrested? Similar questions popped up in my brain within seconds.

"Mr. Randy Cross, you are under arrest for suspected murder."

I didn't speak a word. Actually, I wasn't able to talk. I was all alone. Nobody was there with me. My family was away.

One of the police officers stepped forward and handcuffed me. There were six police officers in total and two cars. They put me in one of the cars and took me to the police station.

I was locked up. One of the police officers started interrogating me. They had CCTV footage of me shooting Michael.

Damn! How did I miss the cameras? *What am I going to do now!?*

I realized this was the end. They had every proof against me, which made it impossible to defend myself. And I didn't want to protect myself either because all I had done was unforgivable. It was the worst, and I had to be punished.

They asked me to get an attorney, but I would not do anything.

I accepted everything that I had done. I told them about all the murders I had committed. From the first murder to the last, I confessed everything. Maybe it was because of my fate, and I had no choice. I had accepted that it was meant to end like that.

I knew what happened to me in the past wasn't fair, but what I had done was worse.

They transferred me to jail. However, the court provided me with an attorney. Nothing was presented in my favor in the court at the first hearing. I accepted all the mistakes in front of the judge. I confessed in front of the court how I murdered all of my targets. I confessed why it happened. I stated how I hate the discrimination and the healthcare system of America. I was angry, and I did all this because I couldn't control my rage anymore.

The judge convicted me for all of the murders, and I was found guilty. It leads to a death sentence. It was inevitable. I had to face the consequences of all my actions!

I was transferred back to the jail.

I was all by myself, sitting in the dark dungeon-like cell. I was convicted as a serial killer. No one was there for me after all the crimes I committed, not my family, not my friends, not even Jason.

What had I turned into? A thought lingered.

I hadn't thought about the consequences when I was becoming a serial killer. I guess I was in a delusion. I thought I was too powerful that I was invisible, but no… I was wrong.

It was too late now. Everything was ruined. Now, it was time for me to wait for the day everything would end.

Chapter 11: The Final Price

It had been four months until I was sentenced to death, and those four months passed in a blink for me because I had accepted my destiny.

I had a couple of days left before my execution. I sat in the cell, like an actual criminal now, paying the final price for my crimes.

It was the darkest phase for me. I had no choice but to repent or redeem. Everything was over.

I was stuck. I couldn't even run away. I felt helpless. All the powers and courage I had before vanished before my eyes.

I was allowed to contact my family under close surveillance. My daughter came to meet me. Everyone was disappointed in me when they learned what I had done. I felt utterly alone because even my family abandoned me. They were disappointed in me.

I talked to my daughter one last time. It was a small interaction during the visiting hours. I had nothing to say in my defense, and she had nothing to say to me, either. My parents, wife, daughter, and everyone did the last goodbye and left.

I don't blame them—I was solely responsible for everything I had done and shouldn't have expected sympathy from anyone.

I tried calling Jason multiple times.

"Jason?"

"Jason?"

"Are you there, buddy? I need you right now."

I got no response.

My brain was numb. It couldn't comprehend the state I was in. Alone... in a dark cell... a prisoner... waiting for my last day.

To be honest, I wasn't scared. I had mentally prepared for it because I knew I had to pay the price for everything. After all, what I did was unforgivable.

Three more days were left until my execution. Those three days felt like an eternity.

It made me think about the young, enthusiastic Randy, who moved to the US with big dreams from Guyana.

I remember it felt like a dream come true when I made it to the US; ever since, my life has changed. I was taken back to the days when I was bullied just for being a black kid who didn't belong to the US. I was never appreciated. I was taken for granted. I lost my self my personality during my battle, enduring bullying and discrimination just because I belonged to a different race. I was always made to feel less of other White kids around me. I was never provided with better opportunities.

All of these things made me resent. I loathed the system. And when I wanted help, I was deprived of it, too. If I were provided with professional mental healthcare, I might have repented and stopped, or I don't know if I should have recognized it myself and stopped.

Ah! I didn't know anything. It was over for me.

Those three days in the prison felt like I was living in hell. My loneliness and my thoughts accompanied me. I had lost all hope and accepted death as my fate.

The days were turned into nights, and just like that, those three days passed.

It was Monday, the day of my execution. I wished to meet my daughter and my family for the last time, but I couldn't. I met my family during the four months and talked to my daughter only twice.

I was granted my one last meal before the execution, and I was allowed to eat anything or ask for anything I wished to. But I didn't want anything quite literally. All the wishes and desires inside of me were dead already.

I had my final meal and was taken to my last destination. The execution room!

I entered the room. It was like a hospital room with an operating table in the middle and belts on the armrest and legrest.

I took my first step into the room, making my way to the table where a lethal injection would execute me. I had two policemen with me, guarding me on my way.

I sat on the table and lay down with my arms and legs in their designated places. One of the police officers fastened the belts on my arms and legs, tightening them so I couldn't move. I was blindfolded so that I couldn't see anything.

That is it. I thought, clenching my fists.

I could hear someone walking toward me with a lethal injection…

"It's over, Randy," I murmured.

***

Milton Keynes UK
Ingram Content Group UK Ltd.
UKHW022226251124
451566UK00006B/142